A Visit From Grandfather Abacus

Story by Keely Hoffman

Illustrations by Ken Bowser

RSVP

**RAINTREE
STECK-VAUGHN**
P U B L I S H E R S
A Steck-Vaughn Company

Austin, Texas

www.steck-vaughn.com

To my family, who encourages me to do things my way,
and to my teacher, Mrs. Janet Lee Hay, who helps keep me
focused on the task at hand. — K.H.

For my children, Kyle and Teal, who created all of the
lovely background and wallpaper patterns in this book.
No, you don't get paid for them. — K.B.

Publish-a-Book is a registered trademark of Steck-Vaughn Company.
Copyright © 1999 Steck-Vaughn Company.
All rights reserved. No part of the material protected by this copyright may be reproduced or utilized in any form or by any means, electronic or mechanical, including photocopying, recording, or by any information storage and retrieval system, without permission in writing from the copyright owner. Requests for permission to make copies of any part of the work should be mailed to Copyright Permissions, Steck-Vaughn Company, P.O. Box 26015, Austin, Texas 78755.

Library of Congress Cataloging-in-Publication Data
Hoffman, Keely.
  A visit from Grandfather Abacus / story by Keely Hoffman; illustrations by Ken Bowser.
    p.   cm. — (Publish-a-book)
  Summary: Laptop, a young portable computer, is visited by Grandfather Abacus, who explains how he makes calculations using his beads and, in the course of his visit, comes to appreciate more modern technology.
  ISBN 0–7398–0051–5
  [1. Computers — Fiction.   2. Abacus — Fiction.   3. Grandfathers — Fiction.]   I. Bowser, Ken, ill.
II. Title.   III. Series.
PZ7.H6754Vi   1999
[Fic]—dc21   98–37708
                                                                                                    CIP   AC

1 2 3 4 5 6 7 8 9 0   03 02 01 00 99 98

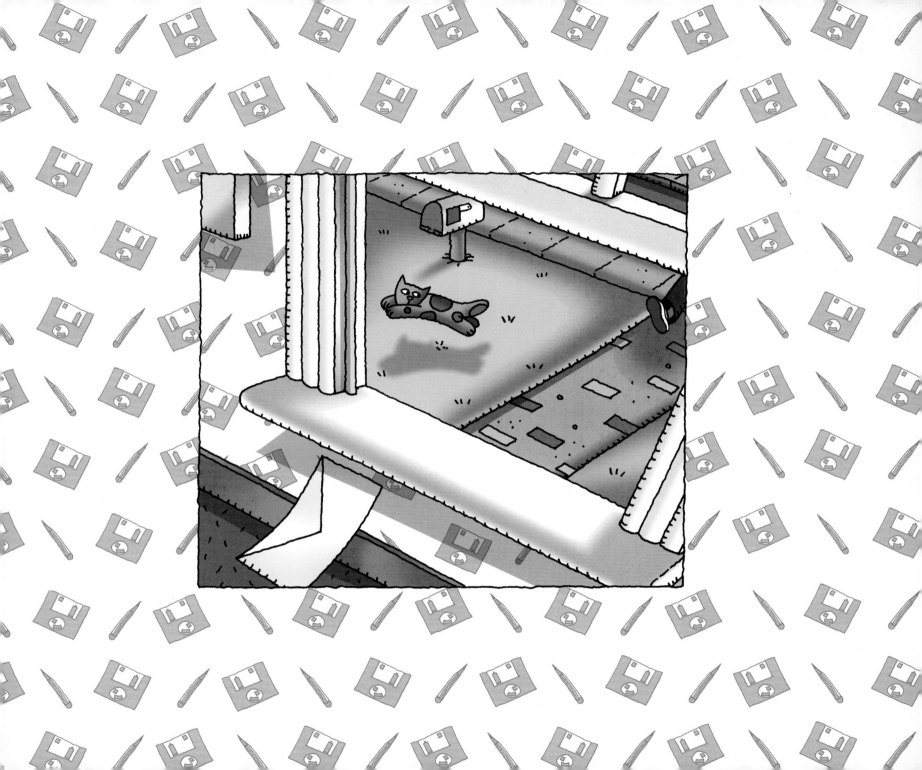

A small portable computer was sitting on a desk in a neat little den. On the screen was the impishly grinning face of a youngster. His nimble fingers were tapping on the keys set into his body.

"Laptop! Laptop!" Mama PC called as she entered the room. "Where is that little computer?"

"Here I am, Mama," piped up Laptop. "What's up?"

"I have a letter from Grandfather Abacus from far away in China," she answered, waving a sheet of paper and a small envelope. "He's coming for a visit."

"A letter! Why didn't he just send an e-mail?" the little portable asked.

"Grandfather doesn't ever use e-mail. He is from a different time where such things were totally unheard of. He is not even electronic," Mama PC explained.

"Not electronic ... how does he operate?" The youngster was clearly confused.

"Grandfather was invented many centuries ago. People used his beads to make calculations," Mama PC smiled.

"Beads? Is that what they called floppy disks or CDs?" Laptop queried.

"No! No! They are ...," Mama PC began as she glanced out the window. "Oh my! Well, you can ask him yourself. He's here! And I haven't even had time to create a file or e-mail Auntie Adding Machine or Cousin Calculator."

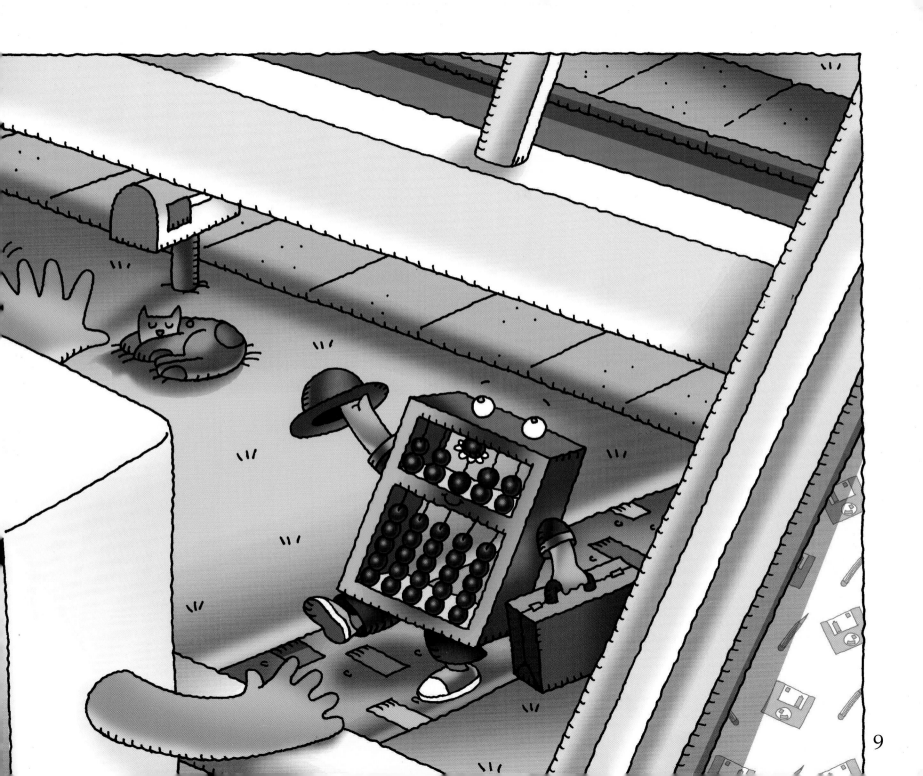

"He's here! Grandfather Abacus is here!" screeched Laptop as he flung open the door. He abruptly slid to a halt. There in the doorway stood the strangest sight Laptop had ever seen. He stared at the rectangular shape with beads that slid on wires between wooden supports.

"Hello, you must be Laptop!" The gentleman at the door greeted him.

"Please come in, Grandfather Abacus," Mama said from behind Laptop. "We just received your letter today, and little Laptop is very excited."

"Yes, he seems a bit stunned." The old apparatus chuckled.

11

Grandfather tried to put Laptop at ease by asking about his family.

"My father is the best. He is the fastest computer around, with a superduper processor and the latest technology ... and ...," Laptop chattered.

But Grandfather Abacus held up his hand. "Whoa, there! I am very happy to see that you are proud of your family, but I must admit I am lost when it comes to all this talk of bytes and RAM and so forth. All I ever needed was my beads."

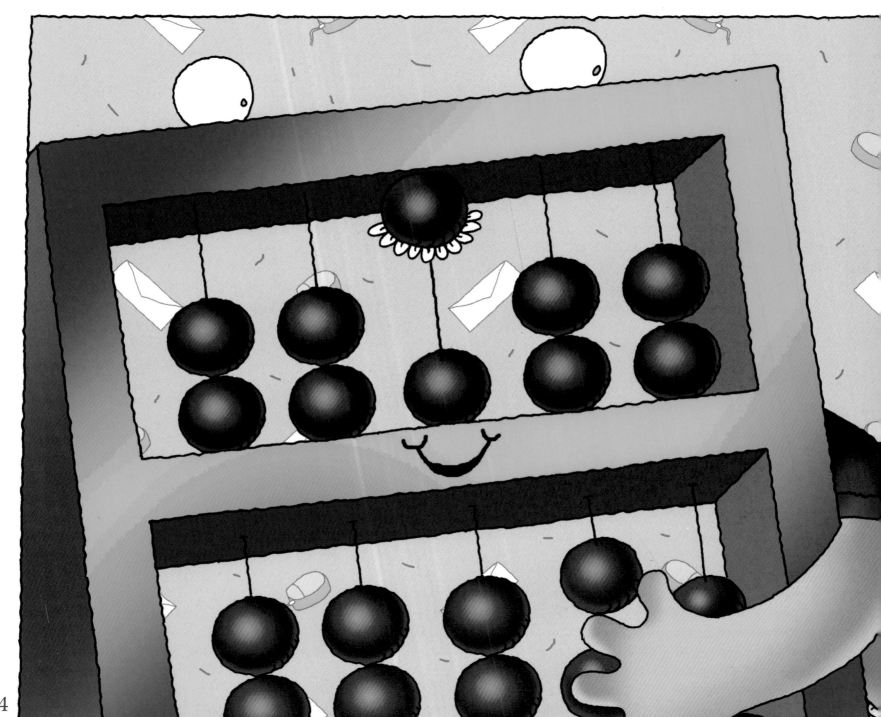

"I do not understand, Grandfather. How were you able to do calculations using only beads?" Laptop asked.

"It is quite simple, really," answered Grandfather. "Each of my wires stands for a different place value, and the beads count out the numerals." He quickly slid beads back and forth over the wires.

Laptop was mesmerized!

"People are lazy today. They should be more like people in my day, when everyone worked their calculations for themselves," said Grandfather.

15

"But, Grandfather, people today also use their abilities. Only now they use them to create machines to help solve their problems." Laptop tried to make Grandfather see the wonder of this new knowledge. However, Grandfather Abacus proved very stubborn. He refused to change his views of technology.

About the time for his visit to end, Grandfather fell off a desk and broke a bead. He became depressed, convinced he was now useless.

"Don't worry, Grandfather, I'll take you to the repair shop. The guys there do really cool stuff!" Laptop said enthusiastically.

Grandfather Abacus was not convinced, but he went along anyway.

The technicians at the shop shook their heads. This just wasn't their kind of equipment.

"I knew it! All this babbling about the wonders of technology was just so much noise. Bah!" Grandfather Abacus ranted.

Laptop was very disappointed.
He was sure the shop could help.
All of a sudden, one of the technicians
gave a yelp. "Wait a minute, let's
check the Internet. I'm sure we can
find some help there."

In a matter of seconds he was
contacting several antique dealers to
find a replacement bead. There was
one right in town. The little computer
and his grandfather were soon on their
way to the store, where the bead was
purchased and installed.

As they left the store and headed
home, Grandfather was very quiet.

"Aren't you feeling well, Grandfather? Sometimes when I'm loading a new program it takes awhile to work all the bugs out," Laptop said, concerned.

"No, it is not that, my son. I am just realizing what an old fool I have been. If it had not been for all this wonderful technology, I would be leaving tomorrow without enough beads to function properly. I am truly grateful to you for all your help."

Grandfather Abacus left for China the next day, vowing to send e-mail to his favorite grandson.

E-MAIL LITTLE LAPTOP

Keely Lynn Hoffman, author of **A Visit from Grandfather Abacus**, was born on August 23, 1986, in Johnstown, Pennsylvania. She has lived all her life in the small town of Somerset. Her father is a lineman for a local electric utility company, and her mother runs a small daycare home and volunteers at Keely's school and many other places in the community. Keely has two older brothers, Heath and Eric, and an older sister, Amanda. In addition, she has a dog named Tyler and a cat named Tigger.

Keely attends Eagle View Elementary School. Her sponsor for the Raintree/Steck-Vaughn Publish-a-Book® Contest was her S.A.G.E. (Somerset Area Gifted Education) teacher, Mrs. Janet Lee Hay, who stresses creative writing in her classroom.

Keely loves to read all kinds of books, especially stories about animals and how people lived in other times. Bookstores are her favorite places to shop. She reports that her whole house is being taken over by books. Keely enjoys music and plays the trumpet, piano, and harmonica. She also enjoys visual arts of all sorts, travel, and Girl Scouts.

Writing is something that she feels she will continue to do for a long time. She began writing daily when she was four years old. Her sister, Amanda, got her started with a Christmas gift of a journal. Keely's future plans are to do something with animals, possibly be a veterinarian. Maybe she'll become the next James Herriot.

In addition to winning the 1998 Publish-a-Book® Contest, Keely was chosen as the recipient of the 1998 Alexander Fischbein Young Writer's Award. This award was established in memory of Alex Fischbein, a writer who died at the age of ten, to encourage young students to write and submit their works for publication.

The twenty honorable-mention winners in the **1998 Raintree/Steck-Vaughn Publish-a-Book® Contest** were Tiffany Chang, Waiakea Elementary School, Hilo, Hawaii; Beverly Nwanna, St. Bartholomew School, Scotch Plains, New Jersey; Jake Horn, Harmony Elementary School, Overland Park, Kansas; Elyse Bledsoe, Green Valley Elementary School, Boone, North Carolina; Joshua Ates, Summerwood Christian Academy, Houston, Texas; Ashley LaPan, Patrick Henry Elementary School, Heidelberg, Germany; Mark Pinske, Trinidad School, Trinidad, California; Meridith Sine, D.L. Beckwith Middle School, Rehoborn, Massachusetts; Rachel Schmillen, Fieldcrest West Middle School, Toluca, Illinois; Ashley Theuring, Ayer Elementary School, Cincinnati, Ohio; Peter Prentiss, Naalehu Elementary School, Naalehu, Hawaii; Kiley Green, La Costa Library, Carlsbad, California; Christy Hough, Sharon Elementary School, Newburgh, Indiana; Frederick Wellborn, Brevard Elementary School, Brevard, North Carolina; Andy Cary, St. Barnabas Episcopal School, DeLand, Florida; Steven Hammes, Waiakea Elementary School, Hilo, Hawaii; Andrea Packer, Salem Christian Academy, Clayton, Ohio; Mark Fox-Powell, The Walden School, Pasadena, California; Bronwen DeSena, Helen Morgan School, Sparta, New Jersey; Michele Lewkowitz, Bayview Elementary School, Fort Lauderdale, Florida.

Ken Bowser has created illustrations for over two hundred books, newspapers, and periodicals. He is married, has two children, and works out of his home studio in central Florida. Oh, and if Kaitlyn asks, he's really been bitten by a shark, he can really pull his thumb off, and he can really see her through the phone.